# BLACK EARTH,
## GOLD SUN

by Patricia Hubbell

illustrated by Mary Newell DePalma

Marshall Cavendish • New York

*For my mother and father—*
*Nanny loved a pretty rose,*
*Grampy loved to grow it . . .*
                    *—P. H.*


*For Julia, Emily, and Will*
                    *—M. N. D.*

Text copyright 2001 © Patricia Hubbell
Illustrations copyright 2001 © Mary Newell DePalma
Marshall Cavendish, 99 White Plains Road, Tarrytown, NY 10591

Library of Congress Cataloging-in-Publication Data
Hubbell, Patricia.
Black earth, gold sun: poems / by Patricia Hubbell; illustrated by Mary Newell DePalma
p. cm.
ISBN 0-7614-5090-4
1. Gardening—Juvenile poetry. 2. Children's poetry, American. [1. Gardening—Poetry.
2. American poetry.] I. DePalma, Mary Newell, ill. II. Title
PS3558.U22 B58 2001
811'.54—dc21   00-052319

*I Know a Tree* first appeared in *The Tigers Brought Pink Lemonade*
by Patricia Hubbell, Atheneum, 1988

The text of this book is set in 13 point Cushing Book.
The illustrations are rendered in watercolors.
Printed in Italy
6 5 4 3 2 1

# CONTENTS

## Spading

The earth's like chocolate cake today—
deep no-flour pure-fudge brownie cake.

Spikey grass frosting
sticks to each slice
I lift and toss.

I run my spade down deep,
fork up delicious earth.
Worm acrobats flip and twist and turn—

*A perfect cake for robins!*

### The Sun and the Marigold Talk to Each Other

"Marigold,
with petals gold,
tell me what you see . . .
Marigold,
with eye of gold,
look up and talk to me . . ."

"Shine down on me
and I will talk . . .
I'll tell you all I see . . .
My roots see blackness,
thick and rich,
my stem sees shades of green—
But O! My eye
sees in the sky
a Marigold—like Me!"

## Bulb Planting

Tip up, grass!
Tip up, worm house!
My trowel is digging a home
For a bare-boned, knobby-kneed bulb.

Soon, winter will sing long songs
To bulb ears,
Songs of buried rainbows
And twirling green kaleidoscopes.

Tip up, grass!
Tip up, worm house!
My trowel is digging a home
For the flashing fireworks of spring.

## In Mary's Garden

Every Johnny-jump-up
Strikes a lively pose—
Bluebells and petunias
Jostle with a rose.

Every flower blossoms there
From every seed she sows—
And everything is neighborly,
And *nothing* grows in rows!

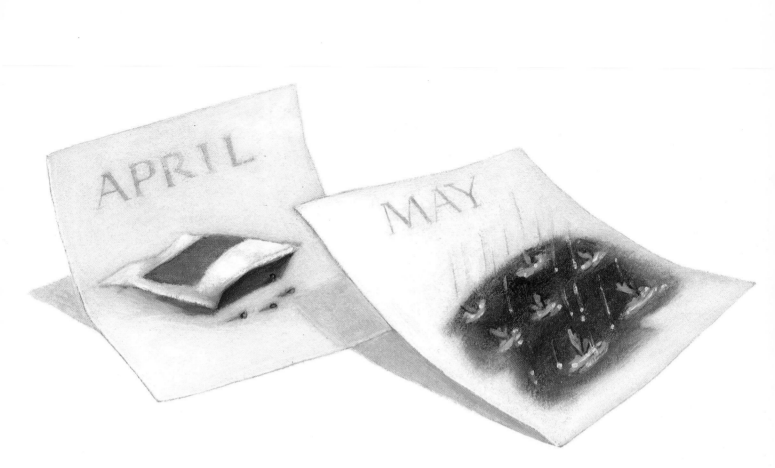

## Planting

In April,
the spinach seeds
roll in their packages,
waiting the touch
of my grandfather's hand.

In May,
in the furrows he makes,
each little lettuce plant stands proud in its puddle.

Now it is June.
Together, we kneel
in freshly turned earth,
planting impatiens and petunias,
marigolds and memories.

## Weeding

Pulling up these frisky little green sprouts
that skip all over my garden
I feel like a traitor,
yanking up the sun's
energy.

> *"Oh, little green sprouts,*
> *you are not the right kind,*
> *your names are all wrong,*
> *you are in places you don't belong."*

Sun hot on my back,
I grit my teeth—
and pile them high.

## Pansies After Rain

Tears, on every face . . .
    And still, you smile!

## Winners

Our
tulips,
held tight
in earth's
dark fist

fight
their first
wind.

Bent low,
they're down—
but not for the count.

Bobbing,
weaving,
they stagger tall,
stand straight.
WIN.

## Dandelions

Sparkling up the grass,
    —Doubloons, everywhere!
Nothing to dig for—
The pirates would love them!

So, how come Papa uproots them all?
How come they shrivel up the gold?
Don't they know about doubloons?

## Why There Are No Blue Roses

When God made the first roses
(white, pink, red, yellow)
He saw conceit shoot up their stems
like sap, and He said:

  "Enough already!
   If I give you blue, too,
   you will be *completely* impossible!"

So He sprinkled it on
forget-me-nots,
whose modesty
astounded
even Him.

## After Lawn Mowing

About a million
little green
trembling stalks
bob up—
and try again!

## Grass

Grass,
    do you hear rain
        beginning in the thunderheads?
Do your roots tingle with the thought of
        dampness, and the clinging dark earth?

Grass, do you know what it is like
    to stand tall as me in the sun,
        looking up at the trees,
           thinking of rain?

Do you wonder, grass, about the birds
    skittering in *your* tallness,
        pecking at your stems?

Do you wonder, grass,
    about the time that is coming,
    when white will cover the earth
and you die down to nothingness?

Do you think, grass,
    about the spring that will follow?
        The sudden bursting colors
           of the shining earth?

Grass, as I lie upon your softness,
    do you feel my body,
        wondering about these things?

## Question for a Hollyhock

Hollyhock,
you
leggy
ballerina,

why
do you
sway
outside
this old
deserted
barn

when you could dance
twinkle-toed
on the New York stage

your
    swirling skirts
        of pale crinkled
            pastel silk

                floating

to a thousand
    clapping
        hands?

# Braggarts

In my garden,
the zucchini think they are hot stuff,
bumping the air aside
in their hurry to get on growing.

Cauliflower!
Pole beans!
Carrots!
Swiss chard!
Peas!
Potatoes!
Lettuce!
Beets!

Each vegetable rushes
into its own space.

The root crops brag
of their knowledge of darkness.
They forget *all* things are anchored
in the blackness
of earth.

## TOMATO

That is your fat red name—
No other suits you.

I think it is the "O's" that do it—
Little suns that remind me
Of summer and of you.

And those two "T's"
as tall and straight
As garden stakes—

Or maybe it's your "M" and "A"
That make me know
How right your name is—
They're like the racks
On which you grow!

It must be everything, TOMATO—
Your whole name—
Each letter makes me think
Of summer, and of salads, and of sun.

## When Writing a Poem About a Carrot

When writing a poem about a
carrot, tunnel its strong core
through crumbling dark 'til
feathery green letters
explode among yellow
butterflies and loudly
buzzing bees.
Bite it.
Listen
to the
c
r
u
n
c
h
!

## Cabbage

Cabbage,
my little green planet,
my sauerkraut,
my coleslaw,
this beetle flying over you
thinks he's an astronaut,
lost in your blue space.

That crack down your side—
Is it the continental divide?
Or the edge of a tectonic plate,
ready to break loose,
plunge you into the dirt of my garden?

## Corn Talk

In the wind,
the corn talks,
stalks bending,
leaves rustling,
silver shimmering.

Each plant
admires its own tassels,
brags of how its ears have grown,
boasts of the depth of its roots.

The plants
whisper warnings
to each other—
*"Full moon tonight—
Raccoon coming!"*
*"Full moon tonight—
Raccoon coming!"*

Their words rush
up and down the rows
as I sit in the dirt of August,
listening to the corn talk.

### Dreaming of Grapefruit

The grapefruit
              are learning to juggle!
        They heave themselves
back and forth     back and forth
      leaves glistening as they rise.

        How can grapefruit juggle themselves?
        Don't they need handlers?
        Why are they wasting their time
        out here in the groves,
        falling, thudding, picking themselves up,
        trying again?

"Hey, listen!" they shout—
"It's grace!   Freedom!   Movement!   Joy!
That great moment
when we pass whirling
through the leaves—
sky, clouds, the whole fantastic earth
turning around us.
        And—we admit it—the cheers of the amazed delight us!"

## Summer Scene

The paddock,
    foaming with elderberries—
My old horse
    walks in beauty.

## The Oak Trees Are Dreaming

It is night
The oak trees are dreaming

In their deep night dream-sleep they mumble

They mumble a windsong of fireflies
They mumble a dreamsong of fireflies

They mumble a windsong of moonfire
They mumble a dreamsong of starfire

| The leaves dream: | dark dreams | thick dreams |
| The trunks dream: | light dreams | fluttering dreams |
| The limbs dream: | deep dreams | tangled dreams |
| The roots dream: | sky dreams | sun dreams |

It is night
The oak trees are dreaming.

## Watermelons

Hide
their secrets
behind cool green.

Split
them open—
What was hidden
is seen;

Pink summer days,
the dark patience
of waiting seeds.

Spit the seeds.
From these small ovals come burgeoning vines, fruit,
another
pink summer day.

## I Know a Tree

I know a tree that blooms at night
with blossoms of gold edged in malachite.

Its odor is nothing like anything other
than tulips in jam or incense in clover.

Its leaves are flashes of silver-gleam.
The veins are ivory. The stems are cream.

The trunk of the tree is slim and sleek,
its wood has the glow of polished teak.

Its roots are tangled and dense and gray
with delicate globules of pale Tokay—

I taste its fruit—so fine, so few—
Roses in raindrops, daisies in dew.

## October Harvest

Now the greengold world
shimmers its spangled dress
and pumpkins lie tumbled
among a weave of vines.

    At night, in the dark wind,
    corn shocks shake
    and mice scurry,
    somersaulting and cavorting,
    riding the pumpkins,
    sliding down their slippery sides,
    squeaking their joy
    to the pumpkin moon.

And into the morning we run,
shouting into the new day,
gathering pumpkins and gourds and Indian corn,
the perfect gold
of October's perfect hours.

## Apple Shadows

Out in the orchard
what do I see?

Apples
and their shadows
high on every tree,

Apples and their shadows
floating in the air,
fat round apple shadows
dangling everywhere!

I pick an apple
from the tree,
I eat it
crunch by crunch—

My apple
and its shadow—
I have them both for lunch.

## Apple

Peeling
this apple,
I feel summer
curl away.

I bite
into icy
whiteness
of winter,
remembering

Scarlet sunsets
fluttering poppies
red sails on white foam.

## Incantation to Night

Let shadow fall across red apple,
Turn apple brown in dappled shadow—
High in tree that owns the meadow
Let the light of evening wither—
Let creeping shadow slip and slide
Over meadow, tree, and apple—
Let the spangled day be gone
And night hang long.

## Night Garden

Beneath the moon
My cabbage grow,
Twenty moons
In every row.

Twenty sunflowers
Close their eyes,
Waiting for the
Sun to rise.

## Dreamers

We are the gardeners
Dreaming our dreams

Dream roots spread deep
Down into the darkness
Of our sleep

Black earth
Gold sun

Our gardens
Our lives

Burst
Into
Flower